Shep
The Turnpike Dog

Written by Charlotte Ann Havey

Illustrated by Renee Gregory

2-2-17

Dream Big!
Best wishes,
Charlotte
Ann
Havey

WELCOME TO
BROOMFIELD
COLORADO

Bear Paw Print LLC

Shep The Turnpike Dog
Copyright © Charlotte Havey 2014

Library of Congress Control Number: 2014935908
ISBN: 978-0-9913406-1-3

First Edition

Printed in the U.S.A.

To Sue Baer, my heartfelt thanks for your guidance and friendship
on this shared journey.

Design and layout by Alysha Havey

To my wonderful and incredibly supportive family, who have helped
me make this dream come true.
CAH

To my mother, Teri Hurst, and my sister, Lisa Swisher, and everyone
else who has taken animals into their homes and families.
RG

Grammy told great stories
From back when she was young.
Shep, The Turnpike Dog
Must be my favorite one.

Playing in her basement,
I found a worn dog collar.
Grammy didn't have a dog.
"Where'd this come from?" I hollered.

With the collar in my hand
I dashed back up the stairs
"Does this have a story?"
"It does," she declared.

"In the 1950's,
Shep was a special dog."
"Tell me," I begged and pleaded.
She agreed with a nod.

"Come on!" she said and grabbed her keys.
"There's a place that we should go."
As we drove, me by her side,
She started, "Long ago..."

They built a road, a turnpike,
To make the traffic flow.
A tollbooth would come later.
The drivers paid to go.

Turnpike builders saw a dog,
A lonely little pup.
Workers spied him, and one called,
"Come boy, drink from this cup."

The day the tollbooth opened
Shep watched cars come and go.
Close he'd circle, then take off,
Too shy to say hello.

When nighttime chased the sun away,
He'd search until he found
A place to sleep under the stars
Upon the cold, hard ground.

Shep dreamed of running with some friends,
Playing a game of fetch.
Early birds chirped good morning,
And Shep woke up to stretch.

One night, a toll taker
Could see a dog outside.
He looked out and called the dog.
"Here boy. Come in," he cried.

Scruffy, without collar or tag,
This dog looked like a stray.
With all his heart, Shep missed a home,
A warm, safe place to stay.

Cold and scared, Shep shivered,
Nervous, ran around.
The tollbooth's lights and warmth
Helped calm that poor dog down.

Shep lapped a drink of water.
Exploring then began.
The tollbooth was a cozy place
Shared with the kindly man.

To say thanks, Shep wagged his tail,
Looked in the man's warm eyes.
He circled 'round, laid himself down,
Breathed grateful, sleepy sighs.

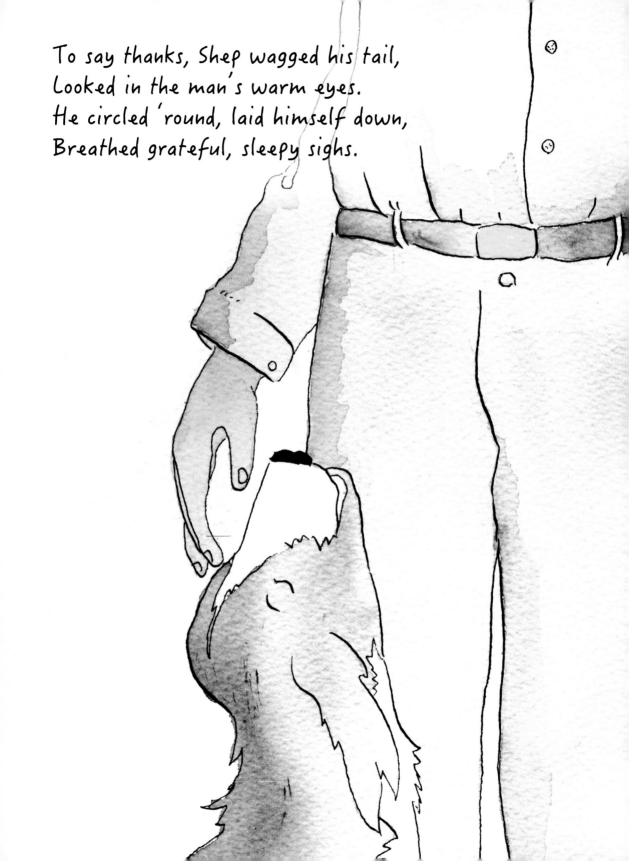

All night inside the tollbooth,
An old coat for his bed,
He felt so safe and happy,
Dreams filled his sleepy head.

When morning kissed the stars goodbye,
Shep dashed out to explore,
Came back to find his friend packed up,
Outside the tollbooth door!

"A dog like you deserves a name.
You look part Shepherd to me.
I'll call you Shep. Yes sir that's it.
Shep's what your name will be."

"Stay now, don't you run away.
I will be back tonight."
Shep wagged his tail and bravely sighed.
He'd stay and wait, all right.

Now near the tollbooth window,
A wooden crate was placed.
Shep jumped up to try it out,
And found his favorite space.

Bright warm days there he would be
Just snoozing in the sun.
Shep, at last, had found his spot,
His homeless days were done.

Perched by the tollbooth window,
Shep barked to say hello
To travelers on the turnpike,
Who slowed to pay the toll.

Spying children in a car,
Shep wiggled with delight.
But when he saw another dog,
He barked with all his might.

A dish, a brush, a collar,
Toys and dog treats, too,
Drivers left at the tollbooth
To say, "Shep, we love you!"

Families took his picture.
His fame spread far and wide.
Like birds in the sky, days flew by.
His friends were by his side.

Shep grew old in the tollbooth.
He could barely see or hear.
One fine day he passed away.
He'd lived there fourteen years!

Grammy said, "That's not the end,
The story goes on here.
At the Broomfield Depot Museum
There's a surprise for you my dear."

"This is a special place,
History and treasures saved."
Beside that old building,
We saw Shep's little grave.

Being there with Grammy,
I smiled at what she'd shared.
The happy tears in her sweet eyes,
Showed me how much she cared.

SHE...

"I love you," she said with a smile.
"This Turnpike story is true.
My father worked in that tollbooth.
I saved Shep's collar for you."

THE END

My story of Shep is based on a true account. From his first appearance as a homeless puppy at a tollbooth on the Denver-Boulder Turnpike in Colorado, to the relocation of his remains nearly sixty years later, Shep is a Broomfield legend. His story connects young readers with a special moment in history and the timeless bond between people and pets.

Dr. Clyde Brunner, a Broomfield veterinarian, donated his services as Shep's personal vet. For many years, a mysterious grave keeper has decorated Shep's grave around the holidays. Shep's legacy lives on in Broomfield today, I hope this special dog's story will be remembered and shared for years to come.

Visit Shep on facebook, www.facebook.com/Broomfield.Turnpike.Dog

Charlotte Ann Havey was born and raised in Colorado and lives there still, dividing her time between Lakewood and Westcliffe. A recently retired educator and animal lover, she wanted to share Shep's story with others. This is her first book for children.

Renee Gregory was raised in Denali Park, Alaska and currently lives in Madison, Wisconsin. She works in the public law sector and loves to travel, read and hang out with her two companions, Miyoko, her cat, and Luc, her dog. This is her first children's book.